TOP SECRET

Valentines

THE PRIVATE PROPERTY OF

....

Top secret Valentines

Top Secret Valentines is filled with everything you need to show those you love how much you care, and it can be kept totally top secret with the special heart-shaped lock!

Take the quizzes to discover your valentine personality, uncover your secret Valentine, and learn all about writing and sending secret messages.

As well as supercute gift ideas for your Valentines, there are beautiful cards at the back of the book for you to decorate and seal using your special stickers!

CONTENTS

SECRET VALENTINE MESSAGES

VALENTINE GIFTS TO MAKE

Valentine *fun facts*

Nobody knows exactly when Valentine's Day started, but one story claims that it was named after a Roman priest (Saint Valentine) who, over 2,000 years ago, performed marriages in secret because the Emperor would not allow it.

By the 1600s, St. Valentine's Day had become a day to celebrate love and friendship. In Britain, children would go from door to door singing songs and asking for cake!

Hundreds of years ago in Europe, men and women would pin the name of their Valentine on their sleeve. This is where the expression "wearing your heart on your sleeve" – which means to let everyone know how you feel – came from.

A red heart is the symbol of Valentine's Day because in ancient times people thought the heart could actually feel love!

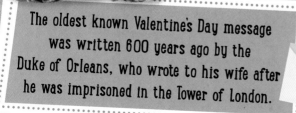

The oldest known Valentine's Day message was written 600 years ago by the Duke of Orleans, who wrote to his wife after he was imprisoned in the Tower of London.

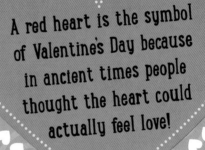

Valentine *fun facts*

Esther A. Howland is known as the "Mother of Valentines." She became famous in the 1800s for starting the first business in America to make fancy, decorated cards.

Teachers receive more Valentine's Day cards than anyone else!

The cards at the back of the book are perfect for sending to your Valentines!

The first special Valentine's Day chocolates were produced by Richard Cadbury, son of the famous British chocolate maker, in 1868.

In Japan, it is traditional for women to give men chocolates for Valentine's Day, not the other way around.

Today, over a billion Valentine's Day cards are exchanged throughout the world each year!

WIL U B MY VLNTINE?

What kind of *Valentine* are you?

Quiet and thoughtful or a fun-loving friend — what kind of Valentine are you? Study the list of activities and choose the five you like the best, then check the large hearts on the right to discover your valentine personality!

Practical jokes ⬭

Dog walking ⬭

Crafts ⬭

Girl Scouts ⬭

Puzzles ⬭

Drama club ⬭

Shopping ⬭

Sleepovers ⬭

Poetry ⬭

Swimming ⬭

After-school clubs ⬭

Concerts ⬭

Volunteering ⬭

Playing an instrument ⬤

Team sports ⬤

Choir ⬤

Parties ⬤

Keeping a diary ⬤

Camping ⬤

Dancing ⬤

Reading ⬤

Drawing ⬤

Theme parks ⬤

Movies ⬤

. . . pink hearts
than any other:

You are a loyal, dependable Valentine who loves teamwork and adventure! You enjoy a challenge and love to win!

. . . red hearts
than any other:

You are a fun-loving Valentine who is always there for her friends whether they need a shoulder to lean on or are looking for fun times!

. . . blue hearts
than any other:

You are a thoughtful Valentine. You may appear quiet but you have a headful of ideas and are super creative!

If, for example, you picked two red, two pink, and one blue heart and can't figure out your type, choose the color of the activity you like best to discover your valentine personality!

Who will be your *Valentine*?

This secret valentine wheel will tell you!

 1 Write the names of **six** possible Valentines under the red hearts around the wheel; these could be friends, celebrities, or even book characters!

 2 Next, write down the following as a list of individual numbers, leaving out any zeros, in the boxes.

- ♥ Your age
- ♥ The day of the month you were born
- ♥ The year you were born
- ♥ Your lucky number (or the one you like best)

Now add all the numbers together, work out the total number, and then fill it in the box. So if you are 12 and you were born on July 23, 2004, and your lucky number is 3, your numbers would be:

Example: | 1 | 2 | 2 | 3 | 2 | 4 | 3 | | | **Total:** 17

My numbers: | | | | | | | | | **My total:**

 3 Finally, starting on the red heart at the top of the wheel, move your finger clockwise, counting the number of small blue hearts until you reach the end of your total number. You may need to go around the wheel a few times!

The name nearest to where you stop is your secret Valentine!

Start

Who will be your Valentine?

The perfect *Valentine*

Draw a heart over the top of three qualities that make up your perfect Valentine. You could keep this a secret or ask your friends to draw hearts around their top three qualities in different colors.

kind

respectful

trustworthy

sporty

dependable

creative

curious

confident

patient

modest

talkative

enthusiastic

caring

Write the names of people who have these top qualities in the small hearts.

12

smart

helpful

calm

funny honest

quiet

tidy

considerate

loyal

outgoing

cheerful

wise

sensitive

charming focused

supportive

witty

optimistic

sociable

My *secret* Valentines

List your secret Valentines and what makes them special here!

Draw or attach a picture here.

Name: ....

School Valentine

Nickname: ....

Most special thing about them: ....
....
....
....

Funniest thing about them: ....
....
....

Perfect date: ....
....

Name:..

Music star Valentine

Nickname: ....

Most special thing about them: ....
....
....
....

Funniest thing about them: ....
....
....

Perfect date: ....
....
....
....
....

My *secret* Valentines

TV & movie star Valentine

Name:...

Nickname: ....

Most special thing about them: ....

....

....

....

Funniest thing about them: ....

....

....

Perfect date: ....

....

....

....

....

Book character Valentine

Name:...................................

Nickname: ....

Most special thing about them: ....

....

....

....

Funniest thing about them: ....

....

....

Perfect date: ....

....

....

....

....

....

Writing

Here are some easy ways to keep your valentine messages super-secret!

Invisible words

Put a piece of paper on top of a magazine, draw a heart on it, then put another piece of paper on top. Pressing down hard so you can see the outline of the heart, firmly write your message on the top piece of paper inside the heart shape.

Give your Valentine a pencil and the bottom piece of seemingly blank paper. You can give them a clue as to how to read your secret message by asking them to figure out the shade of your heart! Shading over the marks on the blank paper with the pencil will make the message appear!

Mirror writing

Writing back to front will make your message more mysterious. Here's how the back-to-front alphabet looks.

Write the message back to front so, for example,
"BE MY VALENTINE" becomes "ƎNITNƎ⅃AV YM ƎB."
Your Valentine will need a mirror to read the message. You can leave them to figure this out, or you can give them a clue by writing "This card is a REFLECTION of how I feel for you!" on the back.

Text and emojis

You can make your message stand out by using text language and emojis. Here are some examples:

Will you be my secret Valentine — becomes . . .

Thank you for being my friend — becomes . . .

You make me laugh out loud — becomes . . .

Friends forever — becomes . . .

will U b my VLNtine? 💀💜

thk U 4 bn my frNd 😊

U mAke me LOL 😂

frNds 4eva 😊

Or try these emojis . . .

 bashful

 cool

 excited

 flattered

 happy

 love

 overjoyed

 romantic

 silly

 secret

 witty

bouquet

celebration

 lovestruck

SECRET VALENTINE MESSAGES

Codes

You can write your message using a secret code, replacing letters with alternative letters or numbers.

Here's an example of a code.

A	B	C	D	E	F	G	H	I	J	K	L	M	N	O	P	Q	R	S	T	U	V	W	X	Y	Z
1	2	3	4	5	6	7	8	9	10	11	12	13	14	15	16	17	18	19	20	21	22	23	24	25	26

Make your own in the grids below.

A	B	C	D	E	F	G	H	I	J	K	L	M	N	O	P	Q	R	S	T	U	V	W	X	Y	Z

A	B	C	D	E	F	G	H	I	J	K	L	M	N	O	P	Q	R	S	T	U	V	W	X	Y	Z

You can give your Valentine a clue to help them read the message. For example:

"To reveal my message, replace each number with a letter
To get you started here's a clue: 1 = A, 4 = D, 10 = J . . ."

Practice writing a secret valentine message here:

....

....

....

Scytale

The ancient Greeks hid messages by writing them on thin strips of material and wrapping them around sticks, a system called the scytale method. You can use a modern-day version to make secret valentine messages!

 1 Cut a strip of paper approximately 12 inches (30 cm) x 0.5 inches (1 cm). Use tape to attach one end of the paper to the end of a pencil, and then wrap the paper around the barrel, attaching it at the opposite end.

 2 Write a short message, using around 12 letters, along the barrel. Be careful to write inside the edges of the strip. Write in pencil so you can rewrite your message in neater letters later.

 3 Remove your message from the pencil and trim off the tape.

 4 Fill in the gaps with random letters.

 5 Write instructions for how to read the message on the reverse of the strip. Try writing it in rhyme, for example:

> "Wrap this around a pencil or stick,
> then discover what makes my true heart tick!"

 6 Attach the message to a small bag of candy like a ribbon, or put it in your valentine card.

Rebus

Many of the first Valentine's Day cards were rebuses, which means that some words were replaced with pictures. This makes the messages seem more mysterious and interesting to read. Try switching these words for pictures in your valentine message.

be = 🐝   can = 🥫   I = 👁   that = T🎩

love = ♥   see = 〰〰〰   my = M👁   you = 🐑

Practice writing messages here.

For example: "I love you" becomes ...

Flowers

Flowers have always been a popular Valentine's Day gift, and many have a secret meaning. Here are some popular flowers and what they represent.

IRIS
wisdom

HEATHER
good luck

CARNATION
beauty

ROSE
love

CHRYSANTHEMUM
optimism

YELLOW TULIP
cheerfulness

POINSETTIA
happiness
and success

HYDRANGEA
sincerity

ORCHID
luxury
and grace

Hidden Valentine

Try hiding your valentine message in a word search. Fill some squares with hearts and flowers.

K	P	♥	A	V	X	Q	T	P
✳	W	I	L	L	♥	Z	O	✳
Y	R	E	V	M	Y	O	U	W
Q	M	A	✳	K	J	B	L	♥
♥	I	B	E	♥	M	Y	H	Z
Z	X	O	R	B	F	W	✳	F
V	A	L	E	N	T	I	N	E
L	♥	V	E	✳	K	R	S	M

Watch your language

Another way to disguise your message is to write it in another language! Here's how you say "Be My Valentine" in different languages:

... French:
Sois ma Valentine

... Italian:
Il mio Valentino

... Swedish:
Var min valentin

... German:
Sei mein
Valentinsschatz

... Spanish:
Va a ser
mi Valentín

... Portuguese:
Seja minha
namorada

Paper fortune cookies

Hide your message in paper fortune cookies that look good enough to eat!

1 On a pretty piece of paper, draw around a plastic drinking glass (one with about a 4 inch [10 cm] diameter works best) and cut out your circle.

2 Next, cut out a thin strip of paper, the same width of the circle, e.g. 4 inches x 0.5 inches (10 cm x 1 cm), and write your secret message on it.

3 Lie your message on top of the circle (towards sides C and D), and then fold sides A and B together, making a half circle – be careful that the message doesn't slip out!

4 Then, using one hand, hold the top of your half circle together (near points A and B) with your thumb and first (index) finger. Now, with the first (index) finger of your other hand, push the bottom of the circle in the middle, bringing sides C and D together with your middle finger and thumb. You should now have a fortune cookie shape!

5 Finally, fasten sides C and D together using one of the small stickers from this book.

Secret-message candy

A jar filled with candy wrapped in secret messages
is the perfect gift for any Valentine!

1 First find a small jar approximately 4 inches (10 cm) tall and enough wrapped candy to fill it.

2 Cut strips of paper long enough to write a message and narrow enough to wrap around the candy.

3 Write messages on the strips. You can say anything you want, but messages about what's great about that person would be perfect! For example: "Thinking about you always makes me smile" or "You're the smartest person I know."

4 Unwrap a candy, then wrap your message, writing-side up, around it. Carefully rewrap the candy and put it in the jar. Alternatively, you can wrap your message around a wrapped candy and then neatly cover the whole thing in aluminium foil.

5 Decorate the jar with ribbons, hearts, and a tag with a valentine message!

For my Valentine

Too-cute candy

Tie small bags of candy or snacks with a ribbon, and then attach a card with a fun message. For example:

Bag of pecans . . .

"I'm NUTS about you!"

Bag of candy bananas . . .

"I'm going BANANAS over you!"

Bag of jelly beans . . .

"I've BEAN thinking about you!"

Bag of mixed candy . . .

"Nothing is SWEETER than you!"

Bag of chocolates . . .

"My heart is CHOC-full of love for you!"

A string of hearts

Make a surprise string of hearts to send in your valentine card!

1 Cut out 8 pieces of stiff red paper, approximately 3 inches x 3 inches (8 cm x 8 cm). Fold them in half and draw half a heart and then a smaller half-heart inside it.

2 Cut out both the big and the small hearts.

3 Using clear tape, attach a piece of thread along the fold of the large heart.

4 Place the small heart in the center of the large heart and attach it to the thread with invisible tape.

5 Fold the sides of the small heart up slightly to create a 3-D effect. Add as many hearts as you want to make a beautiful hanging decoration.

Valentine coupon book

This is a great gift for your parents or bestie!

 1 Cut 12 pieces of paper, approximately 3 inches x 2 inches (8 cm x 5 cm).

 2 Write: "This valentine coupon entitles the recipient to this promise . . ." at the top of each sheet, and then add a promise underneath.

 3 You can have the same promise on each coupon or you could mix them up. Here are some things you could include:

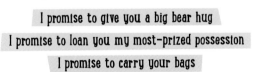

I promise to give you a big bear hug

I promise to loan you my most-prized possession

I promise to carry your bags

I promise to make you breakfast

I promise to polish your shoes

I promise to run your errands for a day

I promise to watch the TV show you love

I promise to help take care of your pet

 4 Draw hearts and flowers around your message.

 5 When you are finished, staple the coupons together to form a booklet and send it with your valentine card!

This valentine coupon entitles the recipient to this promise . . .
I promise to carry your bags.

This valentine coupon entitles the recipient to this promise . . .
I promise to run your errands for a day.

This valentine coupon entitles the recipient to this promise . . .
I promise to watch the TV show you love with you.

TOP SECRET
Valentines
POCKET

Create a secret pocket for your valentine messages!

 1 Cut along the line marked (A).

 2 Next, turn the page and fix the two pages together along the side and bottom.

A

TOP SECRET

Valentines

GUESS *who* IS MAD *about* YOU?

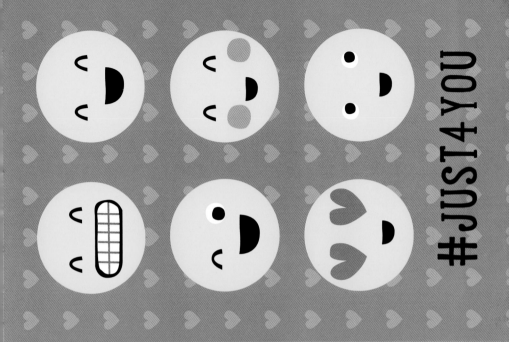

#JUST4YOU

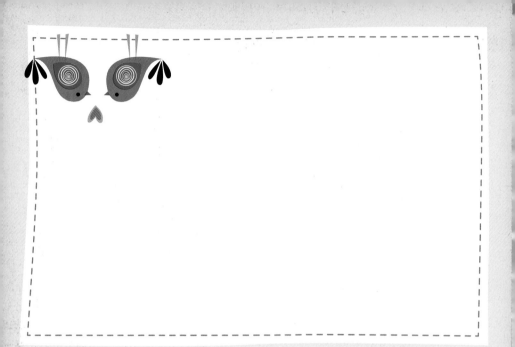

Will you be my *Valentine?*

You're pawsome!